Jim Averbeck

In a Blue Room

ILLUSTRATED BY Tricia Tusa

HARCOURT, INC.

Orlando Austin New York San Diego London

Requests for permission to make copies of any part of the work should be submitted
online at www.harcourt.com/contact or mailed to the following address:
Permissions Department, Harcourt, Inc., 6277 Sea Harbor Drive,
Orlando, Florida 32887-6777.

www.HarcourtBooks.com

Library of Congress Cataloging-in-Publication Data
Averbeck, Jim.
In a blue room/Jim Averbeck; illustrated by Trica Tusa.
p.   cm.
Summary: Alice wants everything in her bedroom to be blue before she falls asleep.
[1. Bedtime—Fiction.   2. Blue—Fiction.   3. Mother and child—Fiction.]
I. Tusa, Tricia, ill.   II. Title.
PZ7.A933816In   2008
[E]—dc22   2006034453
ISBN 978-0-15-205992-7

First edition
A B C D E F G H

Printed in Singapore

The illustrations in this book were done in ink, watercolor,
and gouache on Fabriano 140 lb. paper.
The display lettering was created by Judythe Sieck.
The text type was set in Celestia Antiqua.
Color separations by Colourscan Co. Pte. Ltd., Singapore
Printed and bound by Tien Wah Press, Singapore
Production supervision by Pascha Gerlinger
Art direction by Michele Wetherbee
Designed by Judythe Sieck

For my parents, Larry and Sally, with thanks
for bringing me many safe and peaceful nights—J. A.

For Rob and for Rhe, my world—T. T.

In a blue room,
Alice bounces,
wide-awake past bedtime.

"Time for bed," Mama says,
"and I've brought flowers for your room."
"I can only sleep in a blue room," says Alice.
"Blue is my favorite.
 And those—
 aren't—
 blue."
"Ah . . . but smell," Mama says.

In a blue room,
lilacs and lilywhites
give off a gentle scent.
Alice twirls around,
plops down,
and breathes deep.

Mama returns with a steaming cup.

"Would you like some tea?"

"Blue tea?" says Alice. "There's no such thing."

Mama says, "Just taste."

In a blue room,
orange tea
cools in a brown cup.
Alice takes a sip,
then rubs her drowsy eyes.

Mama brings an extra quilt.
"It's silky-soft and warm."
"It isn't blue," Alice says.
Mama whispers, "Touch."

In a blue room,
a quilt of red and green
feels warm and cozy.
Alice snuggles up.

Mama tiptoes in.

"I have lullaby bells to sing you to sleep."

"Blue . . . ," sighs Alice, "only sleep . . . blue . . ."

Mama smiles.

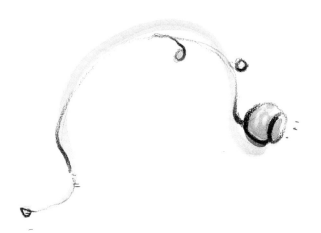

In a blue room,
yellow bells on black strings
chime softly in the window breeze.
Alice yawns,
almost gone.

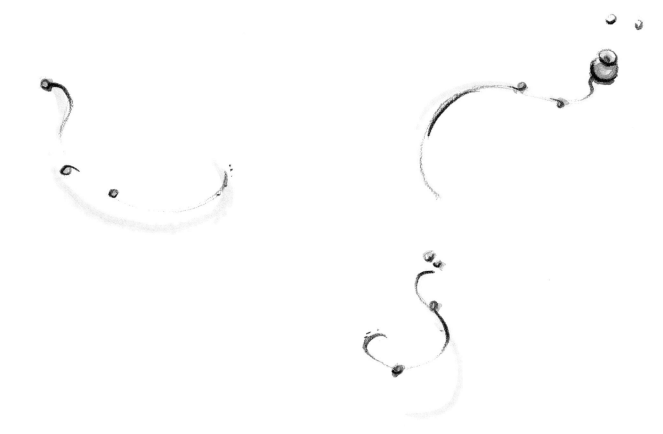

"The moon . . . Mama," Alice murmurs.
Mama whispers, "Here it comes."

Click!

Off goes the lamp and in comes the moon,
bathing everything in its pale blue light.

Blue flowers.
Blue tea.

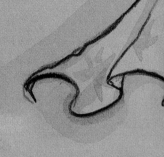

Blue quilt.
Blue bells.

Blue moon.

And Alice, fast asleep . . .

in a blue room.